Where's Eli Moore?

Exploring the Mystery of Carlsbad Caverns

ANNA HAGELE

For Mom, who told me funny stories about garden spiders, butterflies, and baby chicks. I carry them with me like anchors and sails. They are the stories that both keep me rooted and keep me moving forward.

CONTENTS

ACKNOWLEDGMENTS

I would like to thank Miguel for doing such a fantastic job with Eli's field journal sketches, Olya for creating a beautiful cover design, and Noah for providing a thorough edit. I would also like to thank all of my friends and family who have read, reviewed, and aided in the creation of this series. And, of course, as always, I owe boundless gratitude to my husband, Michael, and our four children for their love and support.

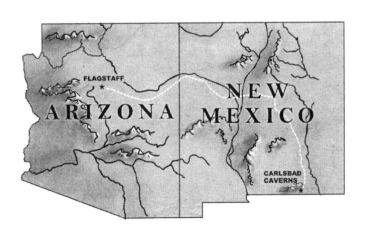

1 BATS

"Eli! Eli! It's time to get up."

"Okay, Dad," I mumbled, sleep still sticking to my foggy brain. I reached over to the table beside my bed and felt for my glasses. I put them on my face and looked at my alarm clock. Three neon green numbers blinked out at me—5:45.

I groaned and rolled over. I closed my eyes and thought about how nice it would be just to stay in bed and go...back...to...sleep.

Wait a minute. I opened my eyes and sat up. I can't go back to sleep. Today is the day of the road trip!

Dad and I are going to the Carlsbad Caverns National Park in New Mexico. I've been preparing for the trip for the last ten days. I've made sure my field journal has

1

plenty of space for new sketches. I've read all about the 400,000 Brazilian free-tailed bats that roost in the caves during the summer. Every night of the summer, right around sunset, they burst forth from the cave and fly out into the desert sky in one long line of hunting bats.

It was finally the big morning. I got up and headed into the bathroom, stopping to pat Kara on the head. She's our sable German Shepherd, which means she is mostly grey. She looks like an unusual cross between a regular German Shepherd and a wolf.

"You better get up soon, girl. I know you like to sleep in, but not today. We are going to go see some bats." Kara sighed, but didn't move from the foot of my bed.

After sloppily combing my hair and brushing my teeth, I got dressed and ran into the kitchen, ready to walk out the back door.

"Hang on, there, adventurer!" Mom said. She was wearing her light blue bathrobe over her pajamas and holding a steaming cup of coffee in one hand and a spatula in the other. "Breakfast!"

I smiled and sat down at the table. I was soon shoving large bites of pancakes smothered with syrup, raspberries, and almonds into my mouth.

Mom shook her head. "Slow down! The bats will still be there if you eat your breakfast like a human being instead of a vacuum cleaner."

Dad was sitting across from me and grinned a mouth full of pancakes at me. Kara sat at my feet and grabbed a few stray bites of bacon that found their way to the floor.

"Are you sure you can't come with us for this one?" Dad asked, holding up his camcorder to get a good shot of Mom.

She put her hands in front of her face. "Not with that thing around your neck the whole time. Just don't get lost in the cave or fall down a hole or something."

Dad laughed, but Mom was only half-teasing. Ever since he started doing his video blogs about rare and interesting animals four years ago, Dad has managed to find his way into quite a few tough spots. He is a biologist and used to spend most of his time in a lab, until he figured out that there was such potential in video blogging.

Dad is, well, a little absent-minded—and a lot klutzy. Since he started on his trips, he's almost fallen into a 20 foot ravine, come a few inches from being bitten by a black mamba (one of the most poisonous snakes in the world) and barely escaped a crocodile

3

ambush.

Yup, that's my dad. Kara is the reason he survived each one of those incidents. She always goes along on his trips.

"Well, at least we won't have to worry about wild pigs at Carlsbad," I said, reminding both my parents about the near miss we had in the Peruvian rainforest earlier this year with a collared peccary.

"Don't remind me. Thank goodness Kara was there to fight it off," Mom said.

Dad reached over to scratch Kara behind the ear. "I don't know what I'd do without her."

The trip to Peru was my first time going with Dad on one of his adventures. Carlsbad Caverns is going to be a breeze compared to the Amazon rainforest.

By 7:00, we were ready. We had already packed our gear into the back of Mom's green Land Rover last night.

Kara gave Mom a big lick on the chin and jumped up into the back seat. I hugged Mom and shrugged a little as she kissed my cheek.

"I know, I know. You think you are too big for kisses from your mom," she said. "Listen to your dad and pay attention to Kara. Most of all, listen to yourself, Eli. May your path be straight and may light always shine upon you."

I hugged her tight. "Love you, Mom and don't worry!" I climbed into the Land Rover and buckled my seatbelt. I waved goodbye to her as we pulled out of the driveway. Dad looked over at me just before he put the car in drive and smiled. "Ready for bats?"

"Yeah! Ready for bats!"

2 SAGEBRUSH AND ALIENS

We drove for hours. On the first leg of the trip through Eastern Arizona, we drove through bleak, blond desert. Everything was dried up and dusty. Even here, however, I noticed that some vegetation grew—tough, spiky looking plants. I imagined if they could talk, they would be rough characters, like a gang of outlaw highway bikers, the only ones who would dare to live in such a desolate climate.

Prickly pear cactus –
Opuntia violaceae santa rita

These plants are tough enough to
grow in the dry hot desert of Arizona.

The land stretched out forever, mirrored by the blue sky which also stretched out forever, and the road which cut a line through both, forever. I drifted away, listening to music through my bright red headphones and imagined that the forever blue sky and the forever blond desert were a forever green ocean.

When I came to, we were leaving Arizona and heading into New Mexico. The land changed from distant horizons to great, sunset-colored rocks rising suddenly from the ground. We went through Window Rock, Arizona, where ancient sculpted arches wrapped around gas stations and tourist outposts. We were soon back out into the dry open desert.

Then, the land changed again. Hills surrounded us, filled with sage and mesquite. We were coming to the foothills of a mountain chain. In the distance, I could see the mountains, their dark shadows cutting the blue sky.

I pointed to the north. "Are those the Rockies?"

"Yeah, the southern end," answered Dad. Suddenly, he stepped on the brake, slowing down. "Look! Look, Eli!"

"What?" I looked out the car windows at

both sides of the road, trying to see what Dad was seeing.

He pointed to the left. "Up there, on my side. Do you see them? Mule deer!"

I leaned over to look out Dad's window. "Oh yeah!" There, standing near a small dirt road underneath a grove of cottonwood trees, were three mule deer.

Dad pointed to the one nearest us. "That one is a male. You see his antlers and how he is bigger than the two females?" I nodded and pulled out my field journal. I already have other sketches of mule deer. They live around Flagstaff, but I had never been quite so close to a male before. They are beautiful creatures with slender, elegant legs under strong, thick bodies.

Dad got out his camcorder and started talking into it. "We are in luck! Before we even arrive at Carlsbad Caverns, we get to see three mule deer, *Odocoileus hemionus*. Notice their large ears that look a bit too big for their heads. That is where they get their name. They are also quite large for deer. These traits separate them from their cousins, the white-tailed deer, which live in central and eastern North America."

We sat and watched the mule deer for a few minutes. They seemed remarkably unconcerned about us, other than the male who paused occasionally to stare at us before nibbling some of the long grass by the road. Then, without warning, he jumped up into the air and bounded across the field, the two females just behind him. I watched them run off. They were gone in seconds.

Mule Deer - Odocoileus hemionus

Large, "mule-like" ears

Large body

Powerful legs

Look at the large antlers!
I've never been so close to a male before.

We kept moving. We left the mule deer and the Rocky Mountains behind and came out again into a land of broad horizons, fields of green and yellow grass. I was struck by how much space there is in New Mexico and Arizona and how much space there must be, then, in the United States, or even in the world. When you drive it all out, you really get a feel for just how *long* the world must be. All of this land is out here, stretching on and on, without even the glimpse or whisper of a human being, just the highway with its painted yellow lines and its border of power cables.

There were some houses, just a few. As we drove down the road, you could see a house coming from a long way off because it was completely alone. I thought about who might live in such a house, such a daring, lonely house out on the edge of nowhere. Some fierce, independent rancher who doesn't need the internet. I smiled at this idea and then frowned when my cell phone blinked out those two dreaded words in the upper right hand corner: No Service.

I soon got bored. My legs were restless and my neck hurt from sitting too long. I sighed. Dad smiled at me.

"Road trip," he groaned. I groaned back. Then, out in the yellow and green grass, I spotted a speck of brown and white movement, and then another and another.

"Dad! What's that?" I asked, pointing to my right.

Dad pulled over to the right side of the road. "Where? Oh, I see! It's a bunch of pronghorn!"

"Oh, yeah!" I could just make out their fawn and white coats. They blended in so well with the grass that I couldn't tell what they were at first. As my eyes adjusted to the way they stood and moved, I could see that there were about twenty of them in the fields, grazing in the early afternoon sun. They were much smaller than the mule deer, like miniature antelopes. Dad got some footage of them and I did some rough sketches.

"Let's stop here to eat. We can watch the pronghorns," Dad said. He opened up the back of the Land Rover and we sat on the back ledge, eating deviled eggs, cheddar cheese curds, and red apples. The pronghorns stayed for about ten minutes and then leapt away, little wisps of brown and white. Kara ran after them and barked, but quickly circled back to the Land Rover.

I laughed at her. "They're too fast for you, girl!" She looked up at me with her tongue hanging out and then turned to smell the long grass. I stretched my legs and climbed once more into the car.

Dad revved up the engine. "Still a few more hours to go!"

Pronghorn - Antilocapra Americana

Horns are just beginning.

Alert ears.

Tan and white coat.

These guys are small, but known for their quick feet. They can run very fast and also very far.

They are known for their endurance and are called the marathon runners of the American West.

Time dragged on. It was late afternoon. I felt sleepy and dazed. There suddenly sprung up along the highway a strange billboard. It was painted black to mimic the night sky and, on top of that background, was a bright green figure with oblong eyes waving at us as we drove by.

"Welcome to Roswell!" was painted in white block letters just above its head. I sat up in my seat.

"Dad! Did you see that? What is Roswell?"

"Roswell, New Mexico—it's a town. Back in the 1940s, there was some sort of aircraft crash that happened on a ranch near there. Lots of people who witnessed the crash believed that it was an alien spaceship. The U.S. government said it was a balloon used for a weather experiment, but the rumors of the alien landing have lasted for over 60 years."

"Wow! Really? What do you think it was, Dad? Aliens or a balloon?"

"Honestly, I don't know," Dad said. "There's a pretty interesting little museum about it in town."

"Can we go?"

"Not today. We've still got over an hour to drive and I want to reach the hotel before it gets too late. I was thinking maybe on the way back we can visit the aliens."

I laughed and nodded. As we drove through Roswell, there were more paintings and sculptures of aliens. Some of them were spooky with weird, empty eyes watching the traffic go by. A few of them were hilarious, little green men with goofy grins. In ten minutes, we left the aliens behind and headed out into sagebrush once again.

For the next hour, the land had more hills and more plants—not only sagebrush, but cactus. We were coming into the foothills of another mountain chain, the western edge of the Guadalupe Mountains. Finally, we drove into Carlsbad just before sunset.

The town was spread out with the main road twisting and turning by fast food restaurants and hotels. It had a desolate, sandy feeling to it even though it was a decent size. The surrounding desert seemed to have crept into the town.

"Hardly seems possible that less than an hour away is an underground kingdom," Dad said. We pulled into the hotel that Dad had booked. We were only staying there for one night, then we would be moving to a campground closer to the park.

I climbed out of the car and groaned. "I

feel like a stale piece of bread."

"Yeah, my knees aren't really working," Dad said, laughing. He walked stiffly around to the back of the Land Rover and almost tripped over a bump in the concrete. Kara barked at him and jumped out of the car.

"It's all right, girl. I didn't fall this time," Dad said, petting her on the head. She sat down and cocked her head. If a dog could roll her eyes, I am sure she would have. I helped get our gear out of the back and we headed into the hotel.

We had cheese enchiladas with spicy green chile for dinner. I had never had such a spicy, smoky sauce on my enchiladas before and I went to bed with the taste of it still on my tongue. Kara, as usual, curled up at my feet in the bed. It felt great to stretch out after the long day of sitting in the car and I was soon asleep. Tomorrow—caves and bats!

3 THE RANGER AND THE RANCHERS

We woke up early, loaded the car, and drove an hour to the park. As we drove through the entrance, we were suddenly surrounded by large hills (or perhaps small mountains) on all sides. The road wound through the valleys between them. They were rocky and grassy at the same time. There were small, dark openings cut out of many of them.

"Look, Dad! Do you see the caves? Do you think the big caves are under these hills?"

"I am not quite sure about the layout of the large caves, but there are certainly caves all over this area," Dad answered.

Within a few minutes, we drove up to the Carlsbad National Park Visitor Center. It was perched on top of the last, largest hill. Beyond it, the land dipped down into a vast valley of blue and brown.

"Wow! What a view!" Dad said. We walked into the visitor center and everyone turned to stare awkwardly at Kara. I smiled sheepishly, hoping that not too many people thought she actually was part wolf.

The visitor center was tall and shiny. It had a newly renovated feel to it. In the center of the lobby there was an amazing sculpture of the Brazilian free-tailed bats in flight.

"Look at that!" I said. The sculpture was made of some sort of dark, pliable metal that looked as if it started as one whole piece and was then carved to create a scene of bats flying in a tornado up to the sky.

"I'm going to find Ranger Adams," Dad said to me. I nodded and turned back to the sculpture. Each bat wing was connected to the next by a narrow piece of metal. I followed the connecting bat wings all the way from the bottom to the top of the sculpture. Then, Dad came back with a tall woman dressed in a ranger uniform. She was even wearing a khaki, wide brimmed hat.

"This is my son, Eli and, of course, as we discussed, this is our dog, Kara," Dad said. "Eli, this is Ranger Adams." I looked up at

Ranger Adams. She had a tanned, stern face. She seemed older than my parents, but also very strong. She looked at me for a moment with sharp eyes and then at Kara. She frowned.

"I told you before, Mr. Moore. It is quite unusual for a dog to go down into the caverns. We will be going into the big room cave first. That is where most of the tourists go. We occasionally have service dogs who go into the big room, but even the most well-trained dogs sometimes get nervous."

"Is the big room where the bats sleep during the day?"

"No. They are in a separate cave, the bat cave. It is off limits to the general public. There is no light allowed and it is usually restricted for scientific study. To bring along your dog and your son is quite unusual. Now, I know, the decision is not up to me. You have gained permission from my superiors to go through with this, but you should know that I have serious reservations about taking a dog and a 10-year-old boy into our bat cave."

Dad nodded calmly. "Of course. I understand your concern, Ranger Adams. But, Kara here has been all over the world in many unusual situations. She has even been in caves before—in Asia."

Ranger Adams pressed her lips together and then turned her eyes on me. "Eli, is it?"

"Yes, ma'm," I said extending my hand to her. She shook it, but raised an eyebrow. "I feel very lucky to have the chance to go into the bat cave, Ranger Adams. Do you think we will see only the Brazilian free-tailed bats or other species? Maybe the myotis?"

I asked this in my best I-am-a-little-scientist voice. In preparation for the trip, I learned that there are actually seventeen different species of bats that live in the park.

Ranger Adams gave me a half-smile. "Well, both the cave myotis and the fringed myotis roost in another part of the cave. We will only be heading down to the Brazilian free-tailed colony today." She sighed. "This way, then."

She led us through the visitor center to a glass door on the side of the building. Dad winked at me and tapped me on the shoulder. Ranger Adams seemed pretty tough, but not too tough for me and Kara to win over. She stopped just before going out the door and looked back towards the lobby.

"Oh, no. Not again," she mumbled. Then she turned to us. "Wait a moment please."

She walked quickly back to the lobby where two people were standing at the information desk. They looked angry. Dad and I followed her a short distance, our curiosity getting the best of us. We stopped about ten feet away and pretended to look at a picture of a huge stalagmite, a rock formation found on the bottom of caves. Kara acted bored. She yawned and laid down on the floor. As I stared hard at the picture, I overheard Ranger Adams.

"That is ridiculous. The bats in the caverns are insectivores. They eat insects, not sheep!" she said.

"But the injuries! The puncture marks! They look like they are from vampire bats!" a man's voice interjected. It was a strange voice, thin and angry and frightened. I glanced over at him. He was wearing a red flannel shirt and jeans with a tattered, yellow ballcap on his head. He was tall and thin and stiff.

"You have to admit, Ranger Adams, this is a disturbing coincidence. Maybe some of the vampire bats migrated with the normal ones. You know, hitched a ride?"

This question was from the other person, a woman. Her voice was deep and round with some laughter in it, much different than the man's. She was small and older than the man. She was wearing a denim dress with a large belt wrapped around it. The belt had a bright silver and turquoise buckle on the front. They were both wearing cowboy boots.

"Very funny, Lizbet, but that is not how it works. Vampire bats don't live or migrate this far north." Ranger Adams replied. Her voice was strong and stern.

"Well, maybe it wasn't the bats. Maybe it was something…else," the man said. He whispered the word "else."

"What is that supposed to mean?" Ranger Adams's voice was cool like stone. There was a pause. Neither of them said anything and then, just barely audible, the man hissed out a strange word.

"Chupacabra!"

"Mr. Puckett!" Ranger Adams exclaimed.

Lizbet cut in, shushing Roy. "Now, now, Roy! Don't be spreading silly rumors. Still, Ranger Adams, we aren't the only ones. There've been half a dozen attacks in the past two weeks, and every one of them has happened within a mile of the park's borders. There's a good chance that something has moved into the park, is killing our livestock, and taking refuge here."

Ranger Adams replied, "I understand your concern. Park rangers are looking into the situation, but as of right now, we have no explanation as to what is responsible for these attacks."

"Well, you better figure it out, Ranger Adams, or we will have this whole place shut down!" Roy raised his voice and a few visitors shuffled quickly away from the information desk.

"Mr. Puckett, please! I am afraid I have a tour today, but if you come to the meeting this evening with all of the ranchers and rangers, we will hopefully be able to come up with a solution," Ranger Adams said.

Lizbet put her hand on Roy's shoulder. "That's fine, that's fine." Roy pulled away from her and stomped his way out the front door. Lizbet took a deep breath. "You know my son, Ranger Adams. He's sort of a hot head. We will come tonight and have our say. Perhaps we can come up with an idea of how to catch whatever is behind the attacks."

"Thank you Lizbet. All of the rangers and I have been doing night searches already, but, whatever it is, it's still escaping us. I will see you tonight," The stone edge in Ranger Adam's voice softened. She sounded tired.

Lizbet followed her son out of the door.

"Sorry about that," Ranger Adams said, coming over to where we were standing.

"Not at all, Ranger Adams. It sounds like you are having some trouble around the park," Dad said. Ranger Adams nodded and looked towards the door where Lizbet and Roy just left.

"I think they are right. There does seem to be an animal taking refuge in the park."

"What do you think it is?"

"That's the thing. It doesn't kill like a mountain lion or rogue coyote and we haven't found any unusual tracks. We will get to the bottom of it, though," Ranger Adams said confidently. She headed back to the side door and we followed her. I looked down at Kara who was walking next to me and wondered if she was thinking the same thing I was…

What is a chupacabra?

4 THE TWILIGHT ZONE

Ranger Adams led us out into the hot desert air. The sun was high and bright and I felt a little bit like a chicken being slid into an oven to bake as we walked downhill along a paved trail. I was wearing a sweatshirt because Dad said it would be cool in the cave, but it was definitely not cool in southern New Mexico.

We didn't have to walk far. Just over the crest of a hill and then, I saw it. The cave entrance! It was a large, gaping hole in the ground suddenly yawning out from the hillside. The path led down and we slowly got closer to the cave. It was soon looming just in front of us.

The path changed from a steady downward slope to a switch-back style. We walked down, back and forth along the side of the hill, going deeper into the cave. When I looked further down, there were people on the trail ahead of us, descending into darkness. When I looked back up the hillside from where we had come, the bright blue sky was behind us. The contrast in up and down, light and dark made me dizzy.

"This is so cool!" I said. I stopped and pulled out my field journal so that I could sketch the strange half-in, half-out perspective that we were standing in. Dad had his camcorder and was talking into it with the cave behind him.

Looking out from Carlsbad Caverns.

"Well, this is it! We have come to Carlsbad Caverns in New Mexico to find the Brazilian free-tailed bats. Kara and Eli are along for the trip!" Dad turned the camera towards Kara and me. I waved and Kara barked, wagging her tail. Her bark echoed and people looked up at us from below in the cave. Ranger Adams waited for us, her face straight and firm.

"Here we go! Into the cave!" Dad said, turning the camera back around to give his viewers the best angle. We headed on further down. There was an increasingly strong, sharp smell coming from all around us. It was so strong that I found it a little difficult to breathe. It made the back of my throat feel scratchy and I coughed.

"Whew! That's intense, huh?" Dad had his t-shirt pulled up over his mouth and nose and I laughed at him.

"Is it the bat guano?" I asked. I had read about the strong vinegar smell of bat poop and wondered if this was it.

"Actually, it's the cave swallows," Ranger Adams replied. "They spend a lot of their time here in the entrance of the cave. Their droppings make the strong smell. We will pass it soon. The bat guano is yet to come."

I looked back up the path. There were

switchbacks above me now that were full of light. I saw the swallows, acrobatic birds diving in and around the cave entrance. They made quick, flickering shadows against the bright sky. One of them dove closer than the others and I watched it carefully as it flew, small and agile. I turned and followed Ranger Adams and Dad, descending further down into the cave.

The entrance to the cave was soon behind us and the space around us was getting darker. I looked back one last time and saw only streams of light coming in from the cave entrance. I could see the trail fine as it was lit by small electric lights along the bottom, but I could only just make out the walls of the enormous cavern we were walking into.

I was shocked at how large and spacious it felt in the cave, as though I was in some sort of grand hall or cathedral with walls of rock and limestone. Still, we kept going down. The air was cooler and wet. The path was slick in places and I had to be careful not to slip. Just as I was thinking about the dangers of slipping off the trail and out into the deep dark of the cave, Dad let out a shout.

"Oh, dear!" He was directly in front of me and I saw his long, awkward legs slip out from underneath him. He landed hard on his butt.

I immediately started to laugh. "Are…you…okay?" I managed to say between laughs. Kara ran up to Dad and grabbed him by the shirt sleeve with her mouth.

"Oh, yes, yes. I'm okay, Kara. I'm not going anywhere," he said, obviously embarrassed. I tried to get my laughter under control and helped Dad up.

"Be careful. The path is slippery," Ranger Adams said dryly. I laughed a bit more.

"Very funny, Eli," Dad said, but then started laughing along with me. He turned his camcorder, which was now on low-light, to himself and explained how damp the trails were and that he had a little "mishap."

We kept walking down the path, which continued to wind down into the strange underground room. We began to see various rock formations all along the side of the trail, each one carefully lit for our viewing. The stalagmites coming up from the floor looked like giant root beer floats that had been frozen in mid-fizzle.

I desperately wanted to touch one, but I knew that I shouldn't. The salt and water and minerals that form the stalagmite wouldn't react very well with the oils on my skin. One touch from a 10-year-old boy probably wouldn't make a huge difference, but if every person who visited Carlsbad Caverns touched it, that stalagmite would probably stop looking like a frozen root beer float and more like just a broken piece of rock.

The stalagmites actually start up on the ceiling with the stalactites. Water seeps down from the up-above, sunlit world through the limestone of the cave. The water gathers minerals as it goes and then drips into the cave.

Over thousands of years, the drips begin to form these sort of rock icicles that hang down from the top of the cave. The rock icicles are called stalactites and they continue to drip water down onto the floor of the cave. The mineral-rich water that hangs out on the floor of the cave slowly builds up into bubbly-looking stalagmites. Sometimes, the stalactites and stalagmites actually meet in the middle and form a column.

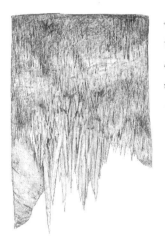

Stalactite - this is the one that hangs from the ceiling and drops water onto the floor of the cave ... the "c" in stalactite stands for ceiling.

Stalagmite - This is the one that comes up from the ground, building up on the drops of water coming down from the stalactites ... the "g" in stalagmite stands for ground!

As we traveled further down into the cave, the path finally leveled out. Ranger Adams paused and turned towards us. "So, we are in what is known as the twilight zone of the cave. Natural light still reaches this level from the cave entrance. We will take a break in about five minutes or so to see if we can find any animal cave visitors."

"Animal cave visitors?" I asked.

"Yes. Many animals take refuge from the heat of the day inside the cave. They usually hide here, in the half light of the twilight zone," she said.

We walked on. I began to make out dark shapes of nearby cave walls to my left and to my right. We had left behind the echoing cathedral and were now in a smaller underground room.

"Let's stop here," Ranger Adams said. There was a small bench on the left side of the path which we sat on. Kara laid down on the trail, at ease even in the dark, dank cave.

Ranger Adams leaned in and whispered to us. "If we are quiet for a while, we might notice something."

We sat still, all four of us. I looked out across the room. The longer I looked, the more I could see as my eyes adjusted to the half-light of the twilight zone. Rocks jutted out at odd angles and everything was painted grey with black shadows. I was reminded of an old picture I once saw of the moon landing back in the 1960s. I was about to mention it when there was a sudden movement to my right, against the back wall of the cave.

Ranger Adams pointed in that direction, then pressed her finger to her lips. We all looked in the direction of the movement. Dad raised his camcorder. There was a side-to-side scuffle along the cave floor from something larger than I expected, about the size of a small cat. It was difficult to see because of the gray light, but I could just make out a pattern of black and gray stripes.

"You are in luck!" Ranger Adams whispered. "A ringtail!" She turned on her light quickly in the direction of the animal and, for a split second, we saw a funny, squirrel-like creature with big eyes, large ears and a long, striped tail. It looked at the light, shocked by the sudden intrusion, and then jumped away back up toward the entrance of the cave.

"Did you get it, Dad?" I asked.

"Yeah, I think so!" He turned the camcorder around to his face and explained that ringtails or ringtail cats are rare to see. They normally live in rocky areas that have access to water and they are omnivores, which means they eat both plants and other animals.

I took out my field journal and made a quick sketch of it although it was difficult to see what I was doing in the shadow of the cave. There was some light from Dad's camera and also from the trail, but not enough to draw well by.

"That was some good fortune for you," Ranger Adams said. "Come along, this way to the big room. There will be more human cave visitors down there."

Ringtail cat - Bassariscus astutus

Big ears and eyes

Really cute Face!

Striped tail

This little guy was hiding in
the "Twilight Zone" of the cave

5 GIANTS AND FAIRIES

We walked beyond the twilight zone. The cave was now dark except for the lights from the trail. I thought about how dark it must be without the lights and I was thankful for the human engineering that allowed me to see the cave all lit up.

We went inside a tunnel of rock. There were green and brown cave pools lit up beside the trail. Dad stopped and got some footage. We came out of the tunnel suddenly and found ourselves standing at the bottom of a dimly lit large room. The cave stretched far, far above my head. I could barely see the ceiling of it. I felt, once again, as though I was in a vast building. I had to keep reminding myself that I was actually underground.

"Whoa! Can you imagine that when we

are up above, we could be walking over caves like this and never even know it?" I asked.

"Here! Come look at this, Eli!" Dad said. We walked quickly now. The ground was level and the path was less slippery. The air was still quite cool, though, and I was grateful for my sweatshirt. We walked up to a map and a crossroad in the trail.

"It looks like the trail loops around to the right and then ends up at the elevators," I said, examining the map.

"Very good, Eli. We will follow this path around the Big Room cave toward the elevators. Just before we reach them, there is a path up and to the left that will take us to the bat cave," Ranger Adams said.

"Yeah, and right up ahead is the Hall of Giants. Come on!" Dad's glasses slipped down his nose and his voice squeaked. I smiled. Yup. He's getting excited.

We quickly rounded the corner and were greeted with an amazing sight, three enormous columns where the icicle stalactites and the root beer stalagmites had joined together reaching from floor to roof.

"Wow!" I said. I had no other words. I felt as though I was in another dimension, an underground forest where rock grows instead of trees. We followed the path further. There were many places where the stalagmites had not quite reached up to the stalactites, but were very close, perhaps only an inch away from joining.

That space between them, that empty air before they touched was somehow magnetic. It reminded me of that feeling you get just before you get a static shock, the vibration that moves through you just before you touch the metal doorknob.

"Look how close they are! How long will it take them to finally reach each other?" I asked about one stalactite and stalagmite that were only centimeters away from touching.

"Oh, only a few hundred years or so," Ranger Adams said.

Wow. A few hundred years to cross a couple of centimeters? Then, I looked at the distance that they had already covered.

"Man, they have been growing for a long time," I said.

Dad nodded. "It's sort of boggling to think of all the time that they have been down here, growing quietly in the dark." My idea of time was suddenly suspended, wiped clean, as centuries of slow growth—reaching upwards, reaching downwards—passed through my imagination.

"Whoa," I whispered.

Dad laughed. "Come on. Let's keep going."

We left the ancient giants behind and I came back to the present. Centuries were too long of a timespan for my 10-year-old mind to understand. I would leave that to the stalactites and stalagmites.

We moved along the trail slowly, stopping every few feet to gawk at each new rock formation while Ranger Adams told us facts about them.

Shortly after the giants, we came across a field of tiny stalagmites that looked as though they were made of my mom's kitchen sponge. They formed small arches and twists and turns. This area was called Fairy Land and I laughed to myself, imagining small, winged creatures flying from one tiny arch to another, living amongst the sponge rocks.

I looked above and saw long spindles hanging from the top of the cave, striped and delicate. These were called soda straw stalactites. Still others formed great thin waves of rock that looked like frozen chocolate or frosting. These were called draperies.

"Hey, look at this!" Dad said, drawing my attention to the right of the trail. The walls of the cave were white and smooth and had rounded holes pushed through them.

"This is called the Boneyard," Dad said mysteriously for the benefit of his viewers. We stood here for a while and I took out my field journal, making a quick sketch of the fragile, bone-like stone. We kept walking around the great space. The loop was about a mile, but the cave itself stretched far beyond the trail. Ranger Adams told us that six football fields could fit into this one cave alone.

Soda straw stalactites

Drapery stalactites

The boneyard

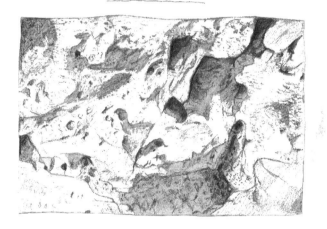

This stalactite and stalagmite are almost touching. It could take them hundreds of years to finally join and form a column!

Close to the end of the loop, there was a wide, dark depth reaching far down into the cave. It was called the Bottomless Pit. When the first explorers discovered the cave, they threw rocks down into the gaping darkness and never heard them hit bottom. This had them convinced that the thing just went on forever.

Eventually, one brave explorer descended into the darkness and found that there was a bottom, about 140 feet below. The reason why they never heard the rocks land was because the bottom of the pit was full of loose soil, which muffled the sound of the landing rocks.

I thought about what it must have been like to climb down here into the dark without a trail, without really knowing where you were going or what might be down here, and then suddenly to walk into this whole other world.

Just before we got to the elevators, Ranger Adams stopped. She pointed to a path that led off to the left. It was small and rough, unpaved and unlit. I wouldn't have even noticed it if she hadn't of pointed it out.

"We will take this path to the bat cave. It is not very far, but we will have to move slow. We cannot use any light on the way as it may disturb the bats. Mr. Moore, you will need to use infrared on your camera and you both will need to wear these." Ranger Adams handed Dad and me masks to place over our noses and mouths.

"The masks are to prevent a histoplasmosis infection. It is a potentially dangerous fungal infection that is found in bat guano." Dad and I quickly placed the masks over our faces.

"What about Kara?" I asked.

"She can get the histoplasmosis infection as well. She will have to wear this special muzzle, I am afraid," Dad said. I looked in shock at Dad. Kara wearing a muzzle?

"It's okay. She wore one when we went into the caves in China and did fine. She doesn't exactly like it, but she manages. Come here, girl!" Dad said. He pulled out a brown muzzle from his backpack and knelt down. Kara came reluctantly over to Dad. She seemed to already know what was in store, but she patiently allowed Dad to strap it on over the back of her ears. She whined after it was on and shook her head. I came over to her and put my hand on her back.

"It's okay, girl. This shouldn't take too long and the muzzle will keep you safe," I said. She looked up at me with sad eyes.

"All right, then. Let's go," Ranger Adams

said. Her voice was muffled by her mask. A small group of tourists passed us by. They quickly moved away from the three masked people with their muzzled dog.

"Now remember, it will be dark. I mean, really dark," Ranger Adams said as we followed the path trail to the left. "We must go slow and careful."

6 INTO THE DARK

We followed the trail which headed up for some time. This was new. The paved path leading from the cave entrance had been either downhill or flat the entire way. The artificial lights from the big room and the elevators gave us some light for a while, but the walls of the cave became more and more difficult to see. Suddenly, Dad made a quick movement in front of me.

"Got it!" He said, grabbing something off one of the nearby rocks and holding it carefully.

"What? What did you get?" I asked. Dad handed me the camcorder from around his neck.

"Get a good view of it, Eli. It's a cave cricket," Dad said. I started recording, and could see it in the viewfinder.

"This little guy is *Ceuthophilus carsbadensis* or the cave cricket. Notice his large hind legs and his super long antennae. These are important because he lives in the low light of the cave. Therefore, he depends heavily on his sense of touch to find food. He eats smaller insects, tiny microbes and, also, other cave crickets!"

Dad gently placed the surprised cave cricket back down on the rock and took the camera back. We watched him for a few more seconds before he jumped away, out of sight underneath the cover of the dim light. Kara whined at the place where the cricket had been, cocking her head, waiting for the tiny creature to appear again.

"Sorry, Kara. He's gone on away from us giants," Dad said.

Cave Cricket - Ceuthophilus carsbadensis

The large hind legs

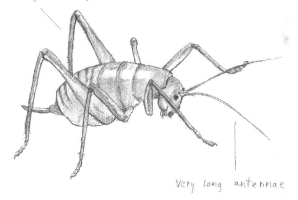

Very long antennae

These crickets use senses other than eyesight
to hunt because they live in the low light
of the cave.

We continued to walk on slowly. The trail leveled off and we entered a low tunnel. The light from the rest of the cave was gone now. The tunnel was very dark and I could see nothing ahead or behind. I automatically put my arms out to the sides, trying to orient myself with the wet rocky walls of the tunnel. The air felt cool and it began to smell again. It was different than the swallow poop smell, more sharp, definitely like vinegar. This had to be the guano. The mask helped, but the pungent air still made me gag.

Suddenly, Ranger Adams stopped. Dad almost bumped into her and I almost bumped into Dad. I had never been in such darkness in all my life. I literally couldn't see my hand in front of my face. I strained my eyes, looking out into the world around me, but there was nothing, no shape, no shadow, no color, only thick darkness. I shivered. Kara moved close to me. I was grateful for my hands and that they could still feel her soft fur since my eyes had failed me.

"Just a little further," Ranger Adams whispered somewhere in front of me. We moved forward and suddenly the sides of the tunnel fell away. I reached out in front of me, trying to steady myself without the cave walls around me. I wobbled a little until I remembered how to stand on my own two feet. I felt the echoes of a great space.

"We are here," Ranger Adams whispered. "Be as quiet as possible." We moved forward a bit further.

I noticed that the ground had changed. It was no longer the firm ground of the path, but a strange, spongy substance. It felt like I was walking on a giant orange peel. I suddenly realized why it felt so weird. We were actually walking on bat guano—hundreds of years' worth of piled up bat poop! Ugh!

I was distracted from my disgust by movement over my head. I felt and heard small flicking and ticking noises, the echo of bat wingbeats. We all stopped for a moment. I looked above me, straining to see the movement of the bats, but failing. My eyes still would only see black.

I closed them and listened, listened to the sounds of the dark world around me, the occasional wingbeats of a thousand sleeping bats and the silence that surrounded them— that deep, cotton-like silence of the dark cave that swallows every hint of sound and light. I was as silent and still as the cave.

Dad tapped me on the shoulder. I opened my eyes, coming back to myself. I could feel Kara's fur next to me and hear Dad whispering. His whisper sounded like a yell in the silence. "Okay, got it. Let's go."

I strained my eyes again, still trying to see even though I knew that I could not. I waited for Ranger Adams to take the lead and I kept my hand on Kara's back, trusting her to lead me out of the darkness. We left behind the spongy ground and the vinegar air, back through the tunnel, and out onto the path leading to the big room.

Even the low light back on the main trail seemed shockingly bright to me now. We all sat down on a bench and took off our masks. No one said anything for a while. We sat quietly. It felt as though I shouldn't speak aloud, that the quiet of the cave demanded me to be quiet as well. I finally broke the silence and whispered, "That was…uh…dark."

Ranger Adams looked back at the bat cave trail. "It is something, isn't it?"

Dad had his hand on Kara's back. "It's funny that it makes you want to whisper,"

"The caves are dark and daunting and so are the bats who call them home. They deserve our respect," Ranger Adams said. Dad and I said nothing. Dad removed Kara's muzzle and Ranger Adams stood up.

"This is where I leave you, I'm afraid. It has been a very great pleasure, Mr. Moore, and also Eli and Kara. I hope that you got what you needed for your video."

"Yes, thank you again, Ranger Adams," Dad said.

"I will see you this evening then, for the bat flight and then our moon walk," She nodded to Dad and then gave Kara and me a rare smile. She turned and walked up the Big Room trail towards the elevator.

7 CHUB AND ROY

Dad turned to me and said, "Well, I don't know about you, but I feel like I need to wash my hands!"

I scrunched up my nose. "I feel like I need to wash my whole body! That bat guano was super gross!"

"It seems like someone should go in there and clean up for the bats sometime. My goodness!" Dad stuck his tongue out in a gagging motion. Kara sneezed in agreement and we both started to laugh. We walked up the trail to the elevators. They were metal and shiny and very out of place in the midst of all the rock and water of the caves. I was relieved, though, to find that my eyes still worked now that there was light to see by.

"Look at the Men's room, Eli!" Dad said

excitedly. I rolled my eyes at him. Only Dad would get excited about using an underground bathroom. Still, the setup was pretty cool. There were two natural tunnels, one leading to the right for the Men's room and the other leading to the left for the Women's. We walked through the Men's tunnel that opened up to a linoleum floor with stalls.

"Weird! Perfectly modern bathroom located in the back of a cave," I said, shaking my head. I thoroughly washed my hands with both soap and hand sanitizer. I even rubbed some on my face and arms.

A fan of Dad's video blogs recognized him and started talking about the seventeen different species of bats in the park. I motioned to him that Kara and I were going to wait outside. I walked away from the linoleum and back into the limestone tunnel. I stopped just before the entrance and leaned against the inner wall of the tunnel, waiting.

Then I heard a voice that was strangely familiar coming from outside of the tunnel. I listened more closely, trying to figure out where I had heard the voice before.

"I did what you told me, Chub. They all think it's an animal that's been killing the livestock." I recognized the voice. It was the rancher from the lobby of the visitor center,

Roy.

"Good, good! Keep it up, Roy-boy, and we will have enough cash to buy our own private island!" Wheezy laughter followed the statement from the unknown man named Chub.

"I even told them it was chupacabra!" Roy said. They both laughed now. Roy's laughter was high and nervous.

"Chupacabra! What a bunch of idiots!" Chub said. "Now, you get upstairs to that meeting. You're ready for tonight, right?"

I leaned in closer to hear Roy's answer, but a large group of people walked by and I missed it. Suddenly, Chub and Roy walked around the wall into the tunnel right where I was standing. They almost ran into me! Roy looked at me for a split second. His eyes were dark and small. He looked pleased with himself, as though he had just done something quite clever.

"Look out, kid!" he said, shouldering his way past me. Kara growled lowly at the two men.

"Young man," Chub said, trying to sound very official. "I don't believe pets are permitted down here. You'll need to go topside." He gave me a stern look and then followed Roy. He had little hair on his head and a round, short frame. He was wearing a dress shirt and slacks. I turned around and watched them disappear down the Men's room tunnel. Dad came out a few seconds later.

"Wasn't that the guy from earlier?" Dad asked. "The rancher?"

"Yeah. I overheard him saying some weird stuff about the livestock and that chupacabra thing," I said. Dad laughed.

"Ah, yes! Chupacabra. That's just a myth, by the way."

"What is it?"

"It's supposed to be a mysterious animal who feeds like a vampire, leaving behind two puncture marks," Dad said. He put his arms out and started talking in a goofy, Transylvanian accent. "I vant to suck your blood!"

"Stop it, Dad! Come on, let's go get something to eat."

We were soon sitting in the little underground snack bar of Carlsbad Caverns, eating turkey sandwiches and nacho cheese chips.

"You have got to see the footage the infrared camera picked up! Look at it!" Dad unstrapped his camera and showed me some of the cave footage on the playback screen.

All I could see was a wide swath of red with a few darting shadows through it.

"What's all the red stuff on the ceiling of the cave?" I asked.

"Those are the bats!" Dad said.

"What?" I asked. I looked again and marveled at the path of red that stretched all across the top of the cave. "All of that is roosting bats? And we were under them?"

"Yup! Amazing, huh?" Dad placed the camera strap back around his neck.

"And we get to see them fly out tonight?"

Dad nodded. "Around sunset. Maybe 7:30 or 8:00."

"Awesome!"

We finished eating and made our way to the elevators. I felt suddenly relieved that we were going back up. I was ready to find my way back to the surface, to sunlight and regularness. The caverns were beautiful, mysterious, magnetic, but also cold and strange.

Dad pressed the up arrow button next to the elevator. "Hey, you were saying you overheard something weird with that rancher?"

"Oh yeah, I almost forgot." I told him what the two men had said.

"Wait. Roy said that he is trying to make

everyone think that an animal is killing all the livestock?" Dad asked.

"Yeah, which probably means that an animal isn't the one doing it," I said.

"Well, if it's not an animal, then it has to be a person."

"Or two people by the name of Chub and Roy," I added.

"Wait. Hold everything. The other guy's name is Chub?" Dad asked. We both started laughing.

"Yeah, Chub and Roy!" I said.

"Ok, but seriously. We have to tell Ranger Adams. This is a big deal. If these men are responsible for the deaths of those animals, they owe the ranchers thousands of dollars."

8 THE LEGEND OF CHUPACABRA

We came out of the elevator back into the main lobby, shiny and new. Dad looked at his watch.

"It's around 5. We still have a couple of hours before the bat flight. Let's try to find Ranger Adams before then," Dad said.

We walked all around the visitor center, but couldn't find Ranger Adams. Dad went up to the information desk to ask where she was. They pointed us to a large conference room behind the information desk. The door was closed, but we could hear raised voices from behind it. Dad stopped just before opening it and raised an eyebrow at me.

"Here we go," he said. Dad gently opened

the door. A small crowd of people were standing in the conference room. There were rows of chairs set up, but no one was sitting down. Ranger Adams was at the front of the group, obviously trying to get everyone to calm down. We walked to the back of the room.

"Please, everyone! Calm down! We must work together," Ranger Adams said.

"Easy for you to say! Your cattle aren't being killed off one by one!" Roy said this. He was standing in the front row, his hands in fists.

"Ranger Adams is right. We need to come together and search for the animal." Lizbet said this, Roy's mother.

"Tonight is a full moon. It might be a good time to search for it as we think, whatever it is, it hunts at night," said a man standing next to Ranger Adams. He wasn't dressed in the typical ranger uniform, but had a brown vest on that read "Ranger in Training" on the back.

"What do you know? You aren't even a real ranger!" Someone sneered from the back of the crowd.

Ranger Adams spoke up. "Mr. Grift is training to be a ranger and he has been very valuable in the search for the animal. He has found tracks near some of the ranches."

"Let's all go tonight, then, and find the thing!" another man said.

"Wait! Wait! Before we all go out there, we should know what we are going after, shouldn't we?" Roy walked up beside Ranger Adams and turned to face the crowd.

"What do you mean, Roy? It's obviously either a mountain lion or a deranged coyote," a voice from the crowd said.

Roy turned back to Ranger Adams. "Tell them! Tell them the truth! You don't know what it is! And the reason why you don't is because it is a chupacabra! Chupacabra has come to haunt us and torment us!"

His voice was suddenly low and mysterious as he faced the crowd. "You all know the stories. My cousin in Puerto Rico swears he saw one! It came at night and sucked the blood of the goats and the cows and the sheep. It leaves two puncture marks in the neck. Just like the ones we have found on our animals!"

There were murmurs from the crowd.

Roy continued. "My cousin says it is small and stands on its hind legs like a kangaroo, but that it has the skin of a lizard and spines along its back!"

"No! You're wrong, Roy! Chupacabra

looks more like a hairless coyote with a spine down its back!" A man from the crowd yelled up. There was a sudden outburst of debate amongst the ranchers.

"Hold on, now, hold on, everyone. Chupacabra is only a myth. There is no scientific evidence to suggest that such a creature exists," Ranger Adams said.

"Then how do you explain the puncture marks?" someone asked.

"I don't know. All I do know is that we need to find the animal responsible before it does any more harm to your livestock," she responded.

"Or to humans," Roy said loud enough for everyone to hear. Everyone started talking at once again. Dad looked at me and motioned to the door. We slipped out unnoticed the same way we came in. Kara was on edge with all of the excited talking from the crowd. She whined as we left the room and sat down on my foot as Dad and I stood just outside of the conference room door.

"Dad! Shouldn't we tell Ranger Adams about what Chub and Roy said?" I asked.

Dad shook his head. "Roy's got those ranchers pretty worked up. Let's wait until we can speak with her in private." We waited outside of the conference room for a few more minutes. Then, some ranchers began to come out. Many of them looked either angry or scared and I got the feeling that the meeting did not end well. Finally, the ranger-in-training, Mr. Grift, and Ranger Adams came out of the door.

"Ranger Adams!" Dad said.

"Oh, hello, Mr. Moore! I am afraid I may have to cut our full moon walk short this evening, but I will at least be able to take you part of the way," she said.

"Oh, that's fine, but we need to tell you something," Dad said.

"I'm afraid that will have to wait, Mr. Moore. I have pressing matters."

"But, Ranger Adams…" I began.

"Sorry, Eli. Can't stop even for you. I will see all three of you after the bat flight." She walked briskly towards the back door of the visitor center.

"I guess it'll have to wait," Dad said. "But, we should tell her as soon as possible. I think she is going to be led on a wild Chupacabra chase!"

We left the visitor center and walked down the path towards the mouth of the cave. It was almost dusk. The bats would soon take flight.

9 BAT FLIGHT

At the mouth of the cave, there was a young ranger I hadn't seen before standing in the outdoor amphitheater. Seats had been carved out of the hillside leading into the cave and most of them were full already.

Dad and I found a seat halfway back and listened to the ranger talk about bats and how they fly. I read all about this before our trip. Bats use echolocation which is sort of like radar. They emit a high pitched sound that bounces off objects and then they are able to "see" the objects or locate them.

Suddenly, just as the ranger was beginning to explain about the hunting habits of the free-tailed Brazilian bats, a shudder was heard from behind her and a cyclone of flying creatures suddenly came twisting out of the mouth of the cave.

The ranger lowered her voice to a whisper. "Well, folks, here we go! Everyone be as quiet as you can and the bats will be more likely to fly directly over our heads!"

I looked behind her and saw small black flecks moving in a circle in front of the cave. As the crowd quieted down, I heard the soft sound of wings, like a flock of birds taking off into the sky, but quieter, deeper and quicker. The bats themselves were noiseless other than the beat of their wings.

They flew in a circle until they suddenly broke off into a great line of black specks moving across the sky over Carlsbad National Park. The sun was setting and the sky was dark blue to the east, where they were headed—a long line of bats flying into the coming night.

The bats might have been noiseless, but the cave swallows who joined in the sunset flight were not. They squeaked and squawked annoyingly over our heads. At first, I couldn't tell the difference between bird and bat as both species were in the air. After about fifteen minutes or so, the swallows seemed to lose their interest in the cyclone of bats streaming out of the cave and moved on.

The bats had steered clear of the

swallows, but now they were venturing further out, right over our heads! I gasped as one of them flew over me and then dove down suddenly. I noticed that they flew differently than birds. They didn't glide along, but instead seemed to fly in angles—straight over, straight down, diving and darting sharply. This must be because of the echolocation. It actually allows them to move more accurately than animals who navigate by sight.

We all sat and watched. I looked across the crowd. Everyone was looking up. There were gasps of surprise and excitement from different parts of the crowd when a bat dove close. The sunset deepened from light orange to red with purple edges. Still, I could see the line of bats flying off through the sky.

The first thing they will do is get a drink in a nearby lake or river because they haven't had any water all day. Then, they will start their hunt, searching for mosquitos and other insects. I watched them, fascinated, unable to break my eyes away from their flight. They just kept coming, a great swarm of them—so many!

Finally, as the sun's last light disappeared and darkness began to dim the edges of my vision, people started moving away from the bat flight arena. Everyone stayed quiet, hoping for another glimpse of a stray bat, as they walked back to the visitor center parking lot and found their cars.

Dad, Kara, and I stayed in the arena. We waited for Ranger Adams. I had almost forgotten about Chub and Roy during the excitement of the bat flight, but now I was wondering again about who or what was killing the ranchers' livestock.

10 MOON WALK

We waited another fifteen minutes. The moon began to rise, full and bright. A figure approached from the top of the arena.

"Ah! Ranger Adams! Eli overheard something that I think you should know about," Dad said, but stopped short when he noticed that the figure was not Ranger Adams. It was the ranger-in-training who we saw earlier at the meeting.

"Sorry, I thought Ranger Adams was coming to take us on a full moon walk."

"That's okay! Ranger Adams was unable to make it. She has some other important business to take care of. But I will be happy to take you, Mr. Moore. My name is Carl Grift. I am a new recruit to the ranger program here," he said, smiling.

"Oh, well, that's fine, but we do need to get a message to Ranger Adams right away. It is very important."

"I can radio her the message if you'd like," Mr. Grift offered, but did not stop walking. He took a path away from the visitor center towards the newly risen moon.

"That would be great. So, Eli here overheard one of the ranchers, that Roy character, talking with another man down in the caves," Dad said.

"Oh?" Mr. Grift left the path and began to descend carefully down into a canyon. "Watch your step here. The bottom of the canyon is the best place to see some of the desert wildlife. Notice how bright everything is in the moonlight?"

"Wow!" I said, looking around. He was right, the rocks and sagebrush surrounding me were standing out in bright silver light. It reminded me of the twilight zone inside the cave, only brighter and under the enormous New Mexico sky. The stars were beginning to pop out, but were dimmed by the full moon.

"You are right about the moonlight! But, I wanted to say that I heard Roy talking with this guy who he called Chub and they were saying that Roy had convinced everyone that an animal was killing the livestock," I said.

"Chub? Oh, that's Charles McFarland," Mr. Grift said. "He's new to Carlsbad, an insurance salesman. Everyone calls him Chub. He's a very nice man, actually. He's given all the ranchers around the park a great deal on insurance because of all of the attacks."

"You mean he is getting everyone to buy his insurance whether an attack has happened on their land or not?" Dad asked.

"Yeah. It's been pretty good business for him, I imagine. Anyway, what's this about convincing everyone that an animal has done the killing? We all know that an animal has done it. How on earth else would you explain it?"

"Well, this might sound kind of crazy, but I am beginning to wonder if this Chub and Roy are working together," Dad said. "Roy attacks the animals and then spreads the rumors about a chupacabra or a mountain lion, while Chub convinces every rancher surrounding the park to buy insurance from him. Then, they split the profits."

"That's a pretty serious accusation, Mr. Moore. I know both Roy and Charles. Granted, Roy has a tendency to fly off the handle, but to take advantage of his neighbors that way? I don't think so. Besides, one of the attacks was at Roy's mother's ranch. He wouldn't do that to his own mother!" Mr. Grift said. "Tell you what. When we get back from the walk, we will go back to the visitor center and I will call Ranger Adams. You can tell her what you thought you heard and she can decide whether or not to investigate, okay?"

I frowned. Mr. Grift obviously thought that the observations of a 10-year-old kid were not to be taken too seriously. Dad looked over at me, his face and glasses lit up by the moon.

"Okay," he said.

"Get your camera ready, Mr. Moore," Mr. Grift said.

We walked on through the canyon until it got very narrow. Then, instead of one wide canyon, we were walking through a series of small, twisting canyons. First to the left, then to the right, then back again.

I was transfixed by the way the rocks looked in the moonlight, bright light, almost white, in contrast with dark shadow. The sky was filled with stars now and there were smoky clouds sitting on the horizon. The world was washed in the moon's pale glow.

"Dad, are you getting this?" I asked. Dad laughed. Kara, however, did not seem to be enjoying herself. She kept shaking her head and fur and yawning.

"What's wrong with Kara?" Dad asked.

"I don't know. She seems to be worried about something," I said, but I was distracted by the moonlight and the difficulty of the trail. It was getting harder to walk in the narrow paths where Mr. Grift was leading us. Kara started to whine and I suddenly sensed that something was very wrong.

Mr. Grift stopped and turned towards us. He was quiet.

"What's wrong?" Dad asked.

"Nothing. Nothing at all. We have come far enough out," Mr. Grift said.

"Far enough for what?" Dad asked. "Is there an animal that has a den near here?" He looked around, panning his camera to the left and then the right. I said nothing, but kept my eyes fixed on Mr. Grift. There was something not right about him.

"No, no animal. We have come far enough out that it will be difficult for you to get back on your own," he said.

Dad laughed nervously. "That's for sure. Not after all of those twists and turns…" Dad stopped talking.

"I knew it would happen eventually. Chub or Roy would give themselves away and we'd have to make a quick exit. It's too bad, really, that it had to be you all."

"Wait a minute. You mean, you were in on it, too?" I asked.

"In on it? It was my idea. I finally had a way to get some quick cash and get out of this hole in the ground," Mr. Grift sneered. "The first death, the one at Roy's mom's place was real. I don't know what kind of animal actually did it, but everybody got so scared and upset about it. That's what gave me the idea. So, I called Chub and told him to move on into town pretending to be an insurance salesman. Then I got Roy to do the dirty work, killing the animals. His family has been ranching this land for years, so he knows the region. I signed on to the ranger trainee program so I could make the whole "animal hiding in the park" story more credible. Worked like a charm until you came to town."

"But, you wouldn't just leave us out here on our own! Not with Eli…"

Mr. Grift interrupted. "Don't worry. You'll be able to find your way back eventually once the sun comes up, especially with that dog of yours. You just won't be back in time to stop us from skipping town. Have a nice walk!" He turned to walk back down the canyon.

Before Dad and I could say anything to

stop him, a sudden loud, sharp call, sad and long, almost like a baby crying, rose over us from the right and echoed along the walls of the canyon. We all froze and looked up towards the scream.

There, full of bright moonlight, stood a huge animal on the edge of the canyon wall, looking down at us. It was an animal that I had only read about and had hoped that I would never actually see up close. A full-grown, adult mountain lion was standing directly over our heads.

11 THE TOUGH SPOT

Things moved quickly and all at once. The mountain lion screamed, gathering itself on its haunches, ready to pounce. Kara started growling, her hackles raised and she placed herself between me and the mountain lion. Dad and Mr. Grift moved away from the edge of the canyon wall just before it leapt. Dad began to yell at the creature, waving his hands up and down in the air.

"Hey, hey, there! Get going, now! We are big! We are not afraid!" he yelled. The animal hissed at him and backed away, suddenly uncertain. Mr. Grift took one look at the mountain lion and ran off into the canyon maze from which we had come. The mountain lion saw the movement and automatically chased after him.

Dad picked up a rock from the canyon floor and threw it at the mountain lion, hitting it square on the back. The mountain lion stopped running and hissed again, shaking itself. It took a long look at Dad and then at Kara who herself looked like a wild animal, snarling and growling, head down, paws wide, ready to jump if the mountain lion got too close. For a few heart-pounding moments, the big cat stared us all down. Then, suddenly, it screamed and lunged towards Kara.

"Kara!" I watched Kara's gray coat flash silver under the moon. She was attacking the mountain lion! With one heavy paw, the cougar knocked Kara off her feet. Kara landed hard on her side and yelped.

The mountain lion was now facing me, growling and snarling. Dad was throwing more rocks and yelling, coming to stand in front of me as Kara had done. I began to throw rocks as well. The mountain lion backed off again, and then suddenly leapt up out of the canyon, clearing a magnificent ten feet in a single bound, disappearing into the night.

Dad and I stood still for a moment, watching the piece of empty sky where the mountain lion had just been. Nothing now. Only the sound of the wind through the canyon and the sight of the open night sky above. I ran over to Kara. She hadn't moved from the spot where she had landed when the mountain lion hit her.

"Kara! Kara!" I sat beside her. She whined quietly and tried to raise her head, but lay it back down again. I placed my hand on her side. Dad sat beside me.

"Dad?" I said. Tears came to my eyes, hot and fearful.

"It's okay. It's okay, girl," Dad was saying, but I heard a small break in his voice. I could feel something warm and sticky on Kara's shoulder.

"She's bleeding," My voice sounded blubbery.

"I know, Eli," Dad said. His hands were also on her.

"We don't…we don't know the way back. Mr. Grift ran away. He left us. We can't get help." My chest felt like someone was squeezing it with a fist and my throat stuck when I swallowed.

"It's okay, Eli. Listen. Take slow, deep breaths, okay?" Dad said in a calm voice.

"Like this. In…" Dad took a deep breath in. I breathed with him. "Then out." He exhaled. I exhaled.

"Good. Now, stay here by Kara and keep

breathing. Talking to her is good. I am not sure how badly she is hurt, but we are going to take a look with my camera light," Dad said.

I nodded. I had forgotten all about Dad's camera. The moonlight had been bright enough that we hadn't used a light on the walk out. Dad turned it on now and a beam of yellow broke through the moonlight. It was strangely comforting. It wouldn't get us back to the visitor center or get help for Kara, but at least we could see her better. Dad shone the light on Kara. I gasped.

"Oh, Dad, it's a lot of blood!" I said, panic rising again within me.

"Breathe, Eli. Remember to breathe. And talk to Kara," Dad said. "It looks like the cougar scratched her there on the shoulder pretty deep. She also hit the ground hard, so she might have a broken rib or two. Feel her feet and legs for any breaks while I search for something to help clean the blood."

I nodded as Dad took away the light. I reached down to Kara's back paws. I squeezed them gently, but Kara didn't wince or whine. They both felt normal.

"It's okay, girl. Good girl," I said. I reached down to her front paws and did the same thing. They also seemed normal.

81

I called over to Dad. "I think her feet are okay."

"Good. Hang on! I am going to keep searching further down the canyon," Dad looked up briefly at the top of the canyon. I knew what he was thinking. He was wondering what we were going to do if that mountain lion came back.

"Call out if you hear anything." He turned around and began to search the ground again for anything that could help clean up Kara.

I looked up at the top of the canyon again. What if it did come back? Even if it didn't, how in the world were we going to find our way out of here? The silver night closed in around me as Dad moved away with the camera light. I was afraid, more afraid than I had ever been in all my ten years.

I thought for a moment about Mom and how she would feel when they told her that we were missing. Tears welled up again in my eyes. Kara moved a little beneath my hands. I tried to concentrate on her instead of my fear. I focused on her breathing and breathed with her.

"That's it, girl. Let's just keep breathing. One breath at a time," I whispered. She whined low.

"Eli! Eli!" Dad called. He was down at the twist of the canyon where Mr. Grift had disappeared.

"What?" I turned towards him. He came running up the canyon so fast that the camera light shook crazily all over the canyon walls.

"What is it?" I asked. He stopped running when he got closer to me, the camera light shining up into his face, reflecting off his glasses. He looked stunned, like he wasn't sure what had just happened.

"You are never going to believe this," he said.

"What?" I asked.

"Mr. Grift dropped his radio." He smiled and raised up his right hand, holding the radio. I laughed out loud.

"You're kidding!"

"No! Can you believe it?" Dad put the radio up to his mouth and held down the call button.

"Ranger Adams, Ranger Adams! This is Peter Moore, over," Dad said. We both waited for a response. Nothing happened. Dad tried again.

"Ranger Adams, are you there?" Dad asked the radio. We waited again. Dad looked over at me, doubt in his eyes. Suddenly, a crackly voice came from the radio.

"This is Ranger Adams, over."

"Aha!" Dad said. He then proceeded to tell Ranger Adams what had happened and that we were stranded with a seriously injured Kara somewhere east of the visitor center in a series of canyons. Relief and hope flooded through me.

I turned back to Kara. "It's okay, girl. You see, Kara? We are going to get you help. Just keep breathing."

Mountain lion - Felis concolor

Black tip of Tail

Tan fur coat

Retractable claws

This guy gave us a real scare and scratched Kara on the shoulder!

12 HEALING AND HUNTING

The next day, Dad and I were sitting in the conference room at the visitor center, the one where the ranchers and rangers had met about the livestock killings. Ranger Adams was sitting across from us at a large table.

"Well, it looks like you three did more than just come to look at bats. You helped us catch a couple of criminals!" Ranger Adams said. As she said this, Kara stood up from beside my chair and gingerly walked over to Ranger Adams.

"Oh, good girl! What a good dog!" Ranger Adams said, stroking Kara on the head. Kara had a pretty close call. She lost a lot of blood from the mountain lion attack and the emergency veterinarians had to give her a transfusion. She also broke some ribs.

But, they sewed her up and other than moving a bit more slowly than usual, she seemed to be healing fine. More than that, she managed to get Dad and me out of the toughest spot we had ever been in.

Chub and Roy were both arrested for fraud. Thanks to Dad's tip to Ranger Adams, she caught Roy in the act of trying to kill a sheep on a local ranch. Carl Grift, however, never returned to the visitor center or his apartment. No one knows for sure what happened to him after he left us in the canyon and ran from the mountain lion.

"You know, it wasn't Mr. Grift or Roy who convinced me that the killings were genuine and done by an animal," Ranger Adams said suddenly.

"Really? What did?" Dad asked.

"Well, now I know this is going to sound strange, but I have been a ranger in Carlsbad for over 20 years. When I first came on, as a young ranger, there were a string of livestock deaths just like these, surrounding the park. The distinctive marking of all the killings, of course, was the two puncture marks on the animals with drained blood. I don't hardly know if anyone remembers it now. The head ranger at the time worried about it and tried to find the animal responsible. We never did figure out what caused the deaths and then they stopped. Just like that. Winter came and we figured whatever it was had moved on. But, when all those animals started dying again, it reminded me," she said.

Dad and I exchanged glances.

"Well, it looks like this time it really was just a human animal," Dad said.

"Yes," Ranger Adams said quietly. She frowned. Kara barked up at her.

"Oh, yes, girl! You are the hero. You all are. Thank you again. You are welcome to come any time to study our bats and our caves. Hopefully next time we can see the myotis species!"

Ranger Adams stood up and shook Dad's hand and then mine. She gave Kara one last pat on the head, put her wide-brimmed hat back on and walked out of the conference room.

Dad smiled at me.

"Well, ready to head back home?"

"Absolutely."

"Yeah, your mom is going to be very glad to get us back."

"She totally freaked out when we told her what happened," I said, remembering the screechy quality of Mom's voice when I told her about the mountain lion.

"Honestly, though, I think she was more worried about Kara than us," Dad said. I laughed. I helped Kara into the back of the Land Rover, more thankful than ever that she's my dog.

"Well, we do have one stop to make on the way back," Dad said.

"Where's that?"

"Roswell, of course. We can't miss the aliens!"

"Aliens? Let's go for it! We've already been this close to chupacabra!"

• • •

Ranger Adams sat in her office and watched the quirky man with his intelligent son and brave dog as they pulled out of the parking lot. She smiled. Then, she looked out over the dusty bluffs of Carlsbad National Park.

It will be sunset soon and the bats will take flight. And Ranger Adams will follow the howl of a strange animal that she has been hearing lately. It sounds a bit like a coyote, but different somehow. She takes a sip of coffee and looks hard out into the west. She will find it. It's only a matter of time.

Here is Kara, our "wolf" German Shepherd

ABOUT THE AUTHOR

Anna Hagele has four kids and she spends much of her time going on pretend and real adventures with them. Just like Eli and his dad, she is an avid animal lover and likes to observe and learn about all of the animals she comes across. She hopes that her books will help kids to open their minds to all of the life around them and to awaken their adventurer spirits.

She lives with her husband, Michael, and their four children in Santa Fe, New Mexico.

Be the first to hear about Eli's next adventure, contests, giveaways, and more!

Join
whereselimoore.com

Like
facebook.com/whereselimoore

Follow
twitter.com/whereselimoore

Made in the USA
Middletown, DE
22 April 2022